Apples and Pumpkins

by Anne Rockwell

pictures by Lizzy Rockwell

SCHOLASTIC INC.

NEW YORK   TORONTO   LONDON   AUCKLAND   SYDNEY

For Lucrezia and Ludovica

ISBN 0-590-45191-X

60 59 58 57 56 55 54 53 52   15 16 17 18 19 20/0

Printed in the U.S.A.   08

First Scholastic printing, September 1991

Lexile is a registered trademark of MetaMetrics, Inc.

When red and yellow leaves
are on the trees,

we go to the Comstock Farm

to pick apples and pumpkins.

Mr. Comstock gives us
a bushel basket
to put our apples in.

Geese and chickens
and a big, fat turkey
walk with us
on our way to the orchard
where the apples grow.

My father picks apples.
My mother does, too.

I climb into a little apple tree
and pick the reddest apples of all.

When our basket is full
of red and shiny apples,

we go to the field
where the pumpkins grow.

I look and look
until I find
the best pumpkin of them all.

My father cuts it
from the vine.

I carry it
back to the car.

At home we carve
a jack-o'-lantern face
on our big, orange pumpkin.

We put a candle inside and light it.
Now our pumpkin looks scary
and funny, too.

On Halloween night
we put our pumpkin on the doorstep.
My mother gives away lots of
our red and shiny apples
for trick or treat,

while I go trick-or-treating
up and down our street.